A FUN
A B C

Sade Fadipe

Illustrated by Shedrach Ayalomeh

A is for Adanah
and my school is on break.

B is for bags
packed with things I'm going to take.

C is for camera
to take pictures of my stay.

D is for Dad
who drives me all the way.

E is for eagles
flying high above the trees.

F is for forest
sunlight shining through the leaves.

G is for gate.
We enter Grandad's yard.

H is for hugs.
I squeeze him really hard!

I is for insects
that dance around my plate.

J is for juice.

I have orange juice with my dates.

K is for kitchen.
I sweep it with a broom.

L is for lantern
sparkling brightly in my room.

M is for mosquito net.
There's one around my bed.

N is for night with lots of stars above my head.

O is for onions
Grandad slices for my eggs.

P is for pump.

We fetch water in our kegs.

Q is for queen.
We make crowns out of hay.

R is for rake.
We clear all the twigs away.

S is for stories
Aunty Sumbo loves to tell.

*T*is for table.

Is that fried plantain I smell?

U is for umbrella.

We love to splash in puddles.

V is for van.

I run to Mum for cuddles.

W is for waving.
Now I feel quite sad.

X is for xylophone.
A gift to make me glad.

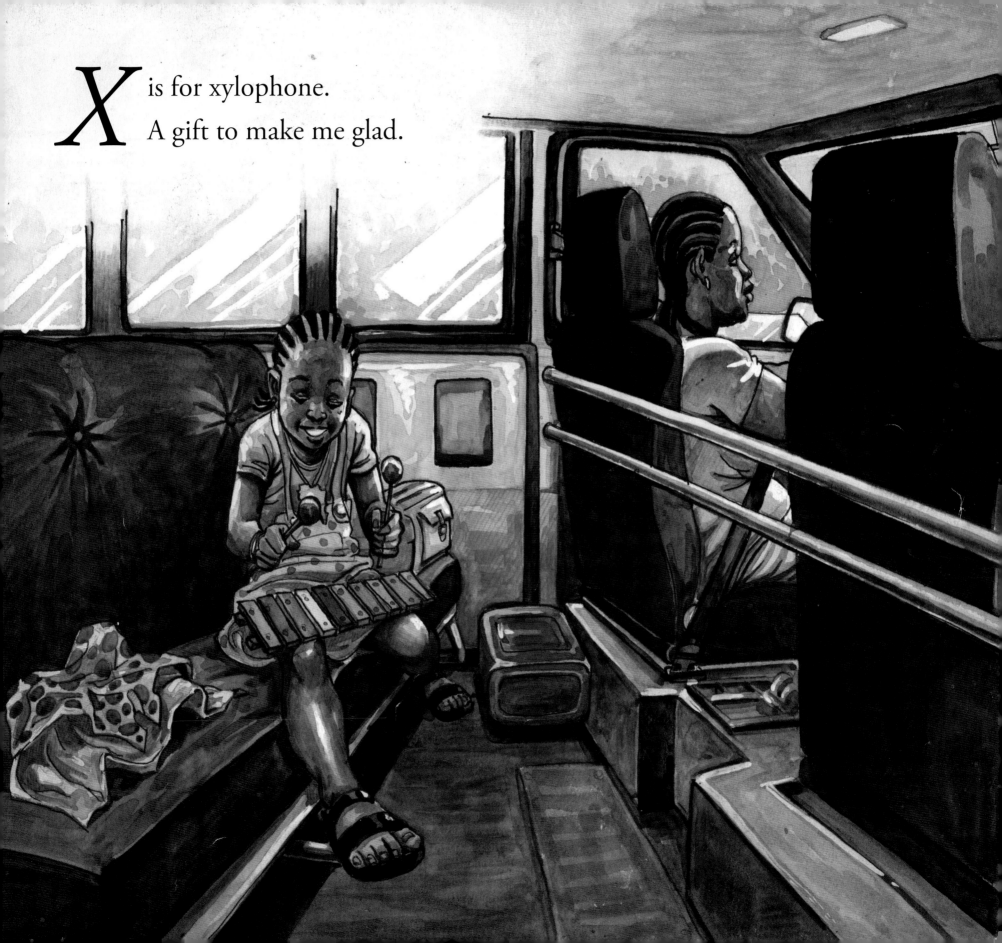

Y is for yams.

Lots of tubers for my mum.

Z is for Zainab.
I hope next time you can come.

A Cassava Republic Press UK edition 2016

Text by © Sade Fadipe 2015
Illustration by © Shedrach Ayalomeh 2015
Edited by Laura Atkins
Design by Charlotte Rodenstedt

A CIP catalogue record for this book is available from the British Library.

ISBN 978-1-911115-15-1

www.cassavarepublic.biz